TRAPPED

DUNSTON'S

CAVE

Caribbean Adventure Series

Book 3

BY CAROL OTTLEY-MITCHELL

ILLUSTRATED BY

ANN-CATHRINE LOO

Carol Mitchell is the author of the Caribbean Adventure Series. In addition to the Caribbean Adventure Series, Carol contributes to online magazines, KittivisianLife.com and NovelSpaces.

Trapped in Dunston's Cave is the third book in the Caribbean Adventure Series.

CaribbeanReads Publishing, Washington DC, 20006

Second Edition
Text © 2011 by Carol Mitchell
Cover and Interior Artwork © 2011 by Ann-Cathrine Loo
Published by CaribbeanReads Publishing
All rights reserved.
Printed in the USA
ISBN-13: 978-0-9908659-2-6
Library of Congress Control Number: 2014919039
www.CaribbeanAdventureSeries.com

TABLE OF

CONTENTS

Chapter 1

Field Trip!

"Trinidad, Trinidad, my Trinidad, my Trinidad!"[1]

Mark sang as he chased his best friend, Kyle around the fountain in the middle of Independence Square in Basseterre, the capital of St. Kitts. He finally caught up with Kyle and grabbed his shirt.

"Got you!" Mark said.

Kyle kept running. Mark held on tightly to Kyle's shirt and was dragged behind him for a few seconds before they both fell to the ground laughing and rolling in the grass.

---

[1] "My Trinidad" by Paul Keens-Douglas from the album "My Daddy".

The boys staggered to their feet gasping for breath. They collapsed on a shaded bench.

Mark dusted himself off. He looked at Kyle.

"Man, you're a mess. Dust off a bit before our parents come out of the meeting. It should be finished any minute now."

"Yeah," replied Kyle. "I can't wait to hear the plans for our school trip."

"It's hard to believe that we're really going," Mark said. "But if your mom sees you now, she'll think she can't leave you alone for half hour, much less for a whole week in Trinidad."

Mark's pet monkey Chee Chee climbed up on to the bench next to him. Mark reached out to scratch Chee Chee's back. The monkey scrambled up on to Mark's shoulder and began to pick at some leaves that were stuck in Mark's tightly curled hair.

Kyle pointed at Mark and laughed. Between chuckles, he gasped "You said *I'm* a mess? Chee Chee's grooming you. He thinks you're a monkey."

"Stop that," Mark scolded, pushing Chee Chee away.

The monkey jumped down from Mark's shoulder and darted away as far as his leash would allow. He sat on a root of a huge flamboyant tree, picking at his long tail and sulking.

Mark was immediately sorry for shouting at his pet. "I'm sorry. Come here boy," he said.

Chee Chee turned and looked the other way.

"I have a special surprise for you," Mark said. "Guess who's coming to Trinidad with me this Easter?"

Chee Chee lifted his small furry head and looked steadily at Mark with his big brown eyes, but still he didn't move any closer.

Kyle exclaimed "You're kidding! Chee Chee is coming with us?"

"Yes!" Mark replied, "You know he stowed away on the bus when we went to Brimstone Hill and then on the plane when we went to Jamaica last summer. So," Mark paused for effect. "Mommy decided that there was no point in trying to leave him behind. We'll get him inspected and everything he needs so he can get on the plane with us … legally this time."

"Woo hoo!" Kyle exclaimed. "That's incredible. We had so much fun with him at Port Royal last summer. Going into the past and meeting pirates like Henry Morgan was awesome."

"Yep, Mommy's been busy trying to get it organized. There aren't any Vervet monkeys in Trinidad, you know, so it hasn't been easy."

Chee Chee had been looking intently at Mark as he discussed the trip. Mark was always amazed at how Chee Chee seemed to understand everything he said. It was obvious that the monkey knew that something good was happening, because he scampered back to where the boys sat and climbed back on to Mark's lap.

Mark hugged the monkey. "I can't leave you behind, Chee Chee. You've been my best friend since I moved here."

"Maybe we'll have another adventure," Kyle said, beaming.

"Maybe we will," Mark said, "but I'm just happy to have a chance to go home. St. Kitts is cool, but I've been here for over a year and I really miss Trinidad."

He tickled the fur under Chee Chee's chin. The boys spotted people coming out of the school hall where the meeting had been held. Mark untied Chee Chee's leash from the bench and the two boys sprinted over to meet their parents. The first adults stopped at the bottom of the steps just as the boys arrived. A man spoke to them.

"Hey boys, all set for the trip to Trinidad? Ingrid is very excited!"

He patted Mark on the back and continued out of the gates without waiting for an answer.

Kyle whispered to Mark. "I hope that wasn't who I *think* it was!"

"It's Ingrid's Dad," Mark replied, bracing himself for Kyle's dismay.

"I thought she said she couldn't come!"

"She signed up too late, but Mommy said Damion dropped out and so she's going," Mark explained.

"She's going to ruin *everything*." Kyle said.

"No she won't. Trinidad is great, and our first stop, the Asa Wright Nature Center is awesome. It's got lots of exotic birds and animals. We can even visit a spooky owl cave. We'll have loads of fun."

Kyle's eyes lit up again and he sang, "Yes, in Trinidad, Trinidad, my Trinidad, my Trinidad."

Chapter 2

Monkey Mischief

The early morning light filtered through the curtains into Mark's room. He was sleeping lightly and the warmth of the sun's rays woke him up. He turned on his bedside light so that he could see in the dim morning light. His clock showed six am. He looked up at the calendar on his bedroom wall. The month of March was almost completely covered in X's where he had marked off the days until their trip to Trinidad.

Mark got out of bed, walked over to his desk and chose a red marker from his pencil case. He drew several circles on the calendar around March 25th. He couldn't believe that the day of their trip was finally here.

Chee Chee sat on the edge of the Mark's desk. Mark met the monkey's gaze, marveling as always at how Chee Chee's dark triangular-shaped face made him look so serious although he really was a very mischievous monkey.

Chee Chee turned and eyed the cage in the corner of the bedroom. Mark had chosen it carefully. It had to be small enough to be taken on the plane as hand luggage, but large enough so that Chee Chee could move around a little. Mark knew that the hardest part of the trip would be coaxing his monkey to get into the cage.

That would come later; first, Mark prepared to leave. He bathed, dressed, ate breakfast and finished his packing. The only thing left was to prepare Chee Chee for the trip.

The monkey watched Mark's every move.

Mark moved towards the cage and Chee Chee moved away. With three long strides he jumped from Mark's desk to the head of his bed, moving as far away from the cage as possible.

He spoke gently. "Don't worry, Chee Chee, it's just for a short while. Then we'll be there. It's the only way you can get to Trinidad with me."

Chee Chee chattered at Mark as if he had other ideas about that.

Mark continued speaking soothingly. "It'll be okay, Chee Chee." Mark bent down, picked up the cage, and placed it on the bed.

Mark straightened up planning to scoop Chee Chee up and put him in the cage. He immediately noticed that the room was strangely quiet. He looked around quickly for Chee Chee but the monkey was nowhere to be seen.

"Chee Chee," he called. "Where are you?"

11

Mark dropped to the floor and looked under the bed. He searched the cupboards, behind the curtains, even in his knapsack, which was where Chee Chee had hidden when he stowed away on the trip to Jamaica. But there was no Chee Chee.

"Mark, it's time to go, come on," Mark's mother opened the door and stuck her head inside Mark's room.

"Aren't you ready? Why isn't Chee Chee in his cage?" she asked in exasperation.

"I can't find him. A minute ago he was on the bed head," Mark pointed to where Chee Chee had been sitting. "But now he's gone!"

"He must be here somewhere."

Mark's mother opened the bedroom cupboards and looking inside.

"He doesn't like the cage. I saw the way he looked at it. He's hiding."

"Could he have snuck out of the door?" Mark's mother asked.

"No, the door was closed until you came in. Where could he be?" Mark banged his hand to his forehead in frustration.

"Well, I hate to say it, darling," Mark's mother said, "but if he's not here, he can't go. Don't worry, when he comes out of hiding, I'll take care of him. Come on, we have to leave now or you'll miss the flight."

"But Mommy, I can't leave him. He was just here, let me look a little longer, he'll come out, I'm sure he will."

"Mark, there's no time," his mother replied.

"I won't go without him," Mark insisted.

"You have to go Mark, don't be ridiculous, this trip is for you, not Chee Chee. If he isn't here you'll have to leave him behind."

"I knew it was too good to be true," Mark said, "going to Trinidad *and* taking Chee Chee along. Man, I promised Kyle that Chee Chee would be there, what's he going to think?"

"Kyle will get over it, Mark. He's not your friend because of Chee Chee, he really likes you. I'm sorry it turned out this way, love, but you guys will have a great time with or without your bundle of mischief. Grab your bag and let's go."

She left the room muttering to herself, "After all the trouble to get permission to take him on the flight, tcah!"

Alone in the room, Mark made one last plea. "Chee Chee, please come out."

He stood in the room waiting for something, some small movement but everything was still.

Mark picked up his suitcase. He thought about how much fun it would have been to have

Chee Chee along on the trip to Trinidad. He had been looking forward to showing the monkey his old home. He took one last look around the room and then, on an impulse, he grabbed the cage and walked out, closing the door behind him.

When Mark arrived at the airport, the other nine children were already there, waiting in a group with the family members who had come to see them off. Ms. Isles, the teacher in charge had collected all of their passports and she was at the counter checking the group in for their flight. The children were excited, talking and laughing loudly.

Mark stood apart from everyone, still upset about leaving Chee Chee behind. He spotted Kyle. His friend was throwing curious glances at the empty cage at Mark's feet. Kyle took a step in

Mark's direction. Mark turned his head away and stepped closer to his mom. He waited, hoping that Kyle would take the hint and leave him alone. He just didn't feel like talking about Chee Chee's absence.

When it was time to go through airport security, Mark said goodbye to his parents.

"Don't fret too much about Chee Chee. Everything happens for a reason," his mother said. "I'll look for him and take care of him."

She reached out towards the cage that Mark held in his hand. "Let me keep the cage since you won't need it," she suggested.

Mark put it behind his back.

"No, mom," he said, "let me keep it. Maybe it will come in handy in the forest at Asa Wright."

"Where's Chee Chee?" Kyle finally had an opportunity to talk to Mark.

"I have no idea," Mark replied, "one minute he was in my room and the next he was gone. My mom made me leave without him."

"Shoot, that sucks," Kyle responded, "Chee Chee is a real strange monkey."

"Yeah," Mark replied, "he's strange, alright."

The children followed their teacher, Ms. Isles, through security procedures and into the departure lounge waiting to board their plane. A few of them wandered around the duty-free shops admiring the souvenirs on sale. The rest sat on the chairs, passing the time chatting, singing or playing hand-clapping games. Mark sat apart from the other children, the cage at his feet.

Suddenly a security guard shouted. "Boy! That monkey has to be in his cage at all times!"

When he heard the word 'monkey', Mark looked up. The man who had spoken was pointing to a spot somewhere behind Mark. He turned around, and sure enough, there was Chee Chee sitting on the back of the next row of chairs, cleaning himself calmly as if he had been there all the time.

"Chee Chee!" Mark exclaimed, and then he ran to where the monkey was sitting. He scooped him up in his arms, pushed him in the cage and shut the door.

Ms. Isles looked up and frowned at Mark, watching to ensure that he secured the monkey in the cage.

"Sorry, sir," he said happily to the security guard.

Ingrid and Kyle walked over to where Mark was sitting and sat on either side of him.

"Where did he come from?" Kyle whispered.

Mark replied "I don't know. He was just sitting there. He must have hid in the car somewhere … and snuck into the airport somehow … somehow." He shook his head, "I have no idea!"

"You know that Chee Chee has to have his own way. That monkey couldn't just walk into the airport like the rest of us. He had to just appear from nowhere." Kyle said.

"He must have changed his mind and decided to join us after all. Maybe this means we'll have another adventure!" Ingrid said her pretty brown face alight with excitement.

"Not WE," Kyle said, "It's Mark's monkey and I'm his best friend, so if anything is going to happen, it'll be him and ME."

"Well, I was in the first adventure at Brimstone Hill," Ingrid replied. She stood.

"Only because you were meddling," Kyle answered.

Ingrid glared at Kyle and stomped off towards the row of seats where their teacher and the other students sat. She stopped suddenly and looked over her left shoulder causing her braided hair to fly around and hit her face. "Well, maybe I'll meddle some more," she said.

Mark interrupted.

"Please, stop it, you two," he said. "We're going to be together for the next seven days, so let's call a truce on the arguing, okay?"

Mark watched hopefully as his two classmates glared at each other for a few seconds.

Then Ingrid sighed.

"I'll agree if you agree," she said. Kyle nodded.

"Now, shake hands," Mark insisted. The two children shook.

Right then, the children heard an announcement asking all passengers to board the plane. They trouped out of the terminal, across the tarmac and on to the waiting plane.

Chapter 3

Asa Wright Nature Center

Mark was relieved that the flight to Trinidad went smoothly. Chee Chee stayed obediently in his cage. When the plane touched down at the Piarco International Airport, Mark felt as if he was going to burst with excitement. He practically ran off of the plane.

He was a little nervous as he took Chee Chee through immigration and customs, but their papers were in order and they were allowed through without any problems.

"We really made it," Mark said to Kyle when they were in the airport's arrival hall. "I can't believe we're really here!"

He looked around at all of the people gathered there to meet their relatives and friends. He realised that he had missed the colourful mix of people that one saw everywhere in Trinidad, descendants of Africans, Indians, Europeans and Chinese. The variety made life more interesting. He was sure that none of his friends were as excited to be in Trinidad as he was.

"Come on this way, Ms. Isles is calling us," Kyle had to grab his arm and pull him towards the bus that had been hired to take them around for the week.

Once they had boarded the bus, Ms. Isles reminded the children of their itinerary.

"Our first stop today will be the Asa Wright Nature Center. We are going to spend one night there. Tomorrow you will be taken to the families who have agreed to host you."

The children looked out of the bus windows eager to have their first glimpses of Trinidad. The road that led from the airport was a highway, wider than most of the roads in St. Kitts. At the end of the highway, they came upon a huge roundabout. The traffic circle was beautifully manicured with neatly cut grass and flowering shrubs. The bus leaned a little as it rounded the corners and the children were tipped to the side. They giggled with delight.

"This is Arima," Mark said to Kyle as the bus turned off of the highway into a town.

The bus maneuvered the busy maze of streets in this town. It was just after midday and people many were about. The children saw houses, schools, office buildings, churches and stores. It seemed that everyday life in Trinidad wasn't so different from that in St. Kitts.

"We're climbing the Northern Range, one of the three mountain ranges in Trinidad," the bus driver announced over his PA system. He had just made a sharp left turn and the bus began its climb up into the rain forest.

The bus hit a deep pothole on the rugged road and Chee Chee, still in his cage, gave a sharp yelp of pain.

"I've got to take him out of the cage or he'll get hurt," Mark said to Kyle.

Mark called out to Ms. Isles.

She was a strict yet kindly woman, had been with them on the trip to Brimstone Hill where Chee Chee had stowed away on the bus. She wasn't very happy about having the monkey on this trip. However, she allowed Mark to let Chee Chee out of the cage after cautioning him to keep the monkey on his leash.

Chee Chee sat happily on Mark's lap and enjoyed the scenery. The air became cooler the higher the bus ascended into the rain forest. The vegetation was lush and the children could see many fields of different crops. Ms. Isles pointed out some of them.

"Those are plum trees and those are cherry trees," she said, pointing to patches of trees heavy laden with red and dark brown fruit.

The children pleaded with Ms. Isles for permission to stop and buy, but she refused.

"It's an hour's drive to Asa Wright so no stops," the teacher said firmly.

They continued on and Ms. Isles pointed out more interesting plants along the way, many of which the children had never seen before. She showed them the yellow and red cocoa pods hanging from the trees in one field and a forest of dark green nutmeg trees in another. They passed steep slopes covered in christophene vines.

Higher up on the mountain side, she pointed at what looked like yellow and orange fields. She told the children that they really were the tops of flowering Immortelles, tall trees covered in brightly colored flowers.

"How high up are we going?" Kyle asked Mark about half way into the drive. "It feels as if we are climbing into the clouds!"

Finally, they arrived at the 90-year old plantation house that housed the Asa Wright Nature Center. The children, tired from their long journey, slowly climbed the stairs to the front of the house. They found themselves on a verandah that was simply and elegantly furnished with rattan tables and chairs laid out for a meal.

The children's exhaustion turned into amazement when they spotted 30 to 40 birds and butterflies hovering and fluttering up and down in front of the verandah. The birds flew around as if dancing to their own raucous medley of singing, cawing and chattering. The children stood looking at the birds with surprise and curiosity.

A large lady wearing a beautiful dress made of colorful batik material crossed the verandah and approached them. Her face was folded into a welcoming smile that caused her ample, rosy cheeks to almost touch her eyes.

"Good afternoon, children," she said.

Mark heard her words in the background, but neither he nor his awe-struck classmates responded. They were too busy trying to touch the hovering butterflies.

"Children!" Ms. Isles said.

The lady laughed.

"Don't be upset with them, Ms. Isles. It is quite a sight and sound, isn't it? Take a closer look over the edge."

The ten children looked over the front of the verandah and then saw why the birds were so plentiful. First, there was a large hedge of flowering plants just beyond the edge of the verandah. Secondly, on the lower level, there were tables laden with food; fruit, nuts, sugar and flowers carefully selected to attract a wide range of animals.

The lady pointed out and named some of the birds. The children recognized a few, especially the beautiful humming birds hovering busily over the flowers. Other names were foreign to the children such as the tame Bananaquit, the beautiful blue Tanagers and the Blue Crowned Mot Mot with its unique racquet shaped tail.

Finally the lady got the children's attention.

"My name is Margaret Howell, but you may call me Auntie Margaret," she told them.

"Good afternoon, Auntie Margaret," the children chorused.

"We're so pleased to have you here tonight." Auntie Margaret continued. "We're happy any time we have an opportunity to teach young people about our work." She paused and looked around, her smile even wider than before.

"Here at the Asa Wright Nature Center, you will see living creatures that you may never have seen before," she continued. "About 15,000 years ago, when sea levels were much lower, Trinidad and Tobago were a part of the South American continent. The islands are now separated from South America by the Gulf of Paria.

"I know that 15,000 years sounds like a really long time," she continued, "but Trinidad still has many plants and animals that are found in South America and are *not* found in any of the other Caribbean islands."

Mark beamed with pride.

Auntie Margaret continued, "Unfortunately, some of our animals are endangered." She paused again and asked, "Do any of you know what endangered means?"

Kyle and Ingrid both raised their hands and waved furiously at Auntie Margaret but she called on Jonathon, a boy who was at the front of the group.

"It means that there aren't many of them left and they may soon all die?" he answered tentatively.

"Right, we have to be sure we don't lose any more of God's creatures. The original owners of this plantation, the Wrights, turned it into a conservation area and donated the land to a non-profit trust. Our job here is to ensure that we maintain the property, over 2,000 acres of protected land and a true sanctuary for the exotic birds of Trinidad. One example is the Pawi Pipile that was almost hunted to extinction."

"Did you have a question, son?" Auntie Margaret was looking at Kyle who had let out a shriek.

"I just saw a weird looking lizard," Kyle responded. "It was gold and black."

"Oh, it's probably a golden tegu. They are beautiful but they can be aggressive, so stay away from them."

Auntie Margaret continued "So later this afternoon, after we get you something to eat, we will be taking you on a short hike to introduce you to the area. Tomorrow morning, we'll put you in two groups so you can explore some more. Unfortunately, we've had to cancel one part of the tour, the visit to the Dunston's Cave where the oilbirds live. …"

Auntie Margaret stopped and pointed at Ingrid who had raised her hand. "Yes, my dear?"

"What are oilbirds?" Ingrid asked.

"Oilbirds are the only nocturnal, fruit-eating birds in the world. They get their name because the babies become quite fat very quickly. When they are just over two months old they are one and a half times *heavier* than their parents. In the past, these fat nestlings were collected and killed for the oil that could be made from heating their fat."

The children gasped in horror.

"That's awful," said Ingrid.

"Yes," continued Auntie Margaret. "Most of the oilbirds at Asa Wright live in a cave called Dunston's Cave. There are just over two hundred birds. Poachers have stolen some baby birds recently, so we have closed activity."

Ms. Isles spoke up. "Poachers? Oh dear, should we be concerned?"

"No," Auntie Margaret reassured her, "there is no reason they would want to hurt anyone once you all follow instructions and stay away from Dunston's Cave."

The children asked Auntie Margaret a barrage of questions about the birds, butterflies and poachers.

Kyle was still tracking the lizard. He whispered to Mark.

"Lend me Chee Chee's cage. I bet I can catch that lizard. I want to get a closer look. The pattern on the skin is really cool!"

"Auntie said to leave it alone," Mark responded.

"I hear you all have brought a monkey with you," Auntie Margaret was saying.

Everyone turned to look at Mark. He stepped forward with Chee Chee on his shoulder and said, "Here he is. His name is Chee Chee."

"Hi Chee Chee," Auntie Margaret said in a friendly voice. Then she warned Mark. "Please ensure that he stays on his leash at all times. I don't want him to disturb our birds or plants and we certainly wouldn't want him lost in the forest."

"Yes ma'am," Mark responded.

He never enjoyed any situation where he was required to keep Chee Chee under control. The monkey always had his own ideas about where he should go and seemed able to get there with or without Mark's permission.

Mark turned to whisper something to Kyle but his friend was no longer there. Chee Chee's cage was also gone. Mark whipped around to his left and right, looking for Kyle but to no avail. He ran over to the edge of the verandah looking out towards the forest's edge, but he still didn't see Kyle.

"What's wrong, son?" Auntie Margaret asked, noticing Mark's agitation.

"I can't find my friend Kyle," Mark replied.

"He must be around somewhere," Auntie Margaret said; however a search of the house and the immediate surrounding gardens proved her wrong. Kyle was no longer in the plantation house.

Auntie Margaret's face was very serious. "We must send out a search party immediately. It will be dark in a few hours and if he *is* in the forest, we have to find him before dark. Between the snakes and the poachers he could be in real danger."

Chapter 4

Lost

"SNAKES!" Ingrid exclaimed. She was now standing next to Mark and she gripped his arm.

"Yes," Mark replied, "Trinidad has four venomous snakes. One of them is the fer-de-lance. That's one of the most dangerous snakes in the world!" Then he noticed how frightened Ingrid was. Her face was pale.

"You don't have to worry in here," he added, "too many people … they won't come here."

"But what about Kyle?" she wailed. "Out there with poachers … and snakes. We have to help him!"

"Auntie Margaret is sending out a search party. I'm sure they'll find him soon. He can't have got far. And you know Kyle. Once he remembers that he's missing lunch, he'll come back." Mark laughed a little, hoping to cheer Ingrid up, but she gave him a withering look.

"Not a good time for jokes, Mark. Kyle and I argue all the time but I don't want anything to happen to him. We should help find him."

Ms. Isles gathered up the remaining children and spoke very firmly to them. "Let's go to our rooms and settle in until Kyle is found. I need everyone to stay together; no one else is to wander off."

Ingrid raised her hand. "Ms. Isles, can Mark and I please wait here for Kyle? We're his best friends, and we want to be here when he gets back."

Ms. Isles looked at the innocent, pleading expression on Ingrid's face and gave in. "Okay, just make sure that you both stay put on the verandah. No wandering off, I'll be back soon."

Mark and Ingrid agreed and then continued their argument in whispers.

Mark said "I want him back just as much as you do, but that's a job for the experts. Better if we wait here. Plus, we just promised Ms. Isles."

Mark looked at from Ingrid. He could see a spark growing in her eyes, a sure sign that she was about to get them both into trouble.

"You can't just stay here doing nothing; he's your best friend!" Ingrid insisted.

"I can, just watch me. I told him not to go chasing the stupid lizard anyway," Mark said defiantly. Then he dropped his head. "I really hope he's okay."

"There's only one way to find out. We'll take Chee Chee and go looking for Kyle. Chee Chee will warn us of any danger," Ingrid said authoritatively.

Mark sighed. "Okay, we'll just go down to the forest's edge, just to the edge that we can see from here. We'll see if Chee Chee can pick up his scent. Vervet monkeys are supposed to have a good sense of smell."

They headed down the steps and towards the trees below. The two children immediately understood how Kyle could have been drawn into the fascinating rain forest. There were a large variety of trees and flowering plants of all shapes and sizes.

Mark recognized the ginger lilies, but he was more interested in the trumpet-shaped flowers that he spotted in abundance. The birds continued their loud chorus and butterflies fluttered from plant to plant, spots of colour moving in the lush green. Mark wished that he could identify even a few of the bird calls that he heard.

They immediately forgot their promise to Ms. Isles and their plan to go only to the forest's edge. There was a well worn path and Ingrid started down it confidently. Mark and Chee Chee followed.

The path was wide; wide enough for the children to walk side by side but Mark stayed behind Ingrid. He stopped whenever he saw a creature. He saw many: preying mantis, stick insects, lizards and tree frogs. He often strayed off of the path, fell behind and had to run to catch up with Ingrid. She followed the path, her eyes fixed on the ground watching her step.

After walking for about five minutes, Ingrid stopped suddenly. Mark, who was right behind her, had to step back to avoid running into her back.

"What was that?!" she asked.

"I didn't hear anything," Mark replied.

"Shhh. Listen."

This time Mark heard the knocking sound. It came from his left. He looked quickly around and the sound stopped. He took two steps forward and it started again. Rat-tat-tat-tat-tat.

"What is it?" Ingrid asked. She was also looking around the trees.

Finally Mark spotted the culprit. A chestnut colored woodpecker with red cheeks and a streak of light brown on his head firmly gripped a small tree trunk and hammered away happily at it.

"There it is. A woodpecker." Mark cried, pointing at the bird. "How cool is that?"

Ingrid looked over his shoulder.

"Oh!" she exclaimed, "Beautiful!"

They looked at the bird for a few seconds. It totally ignored them as it focused on its job, tapping at the tree, pausing and then tapping some more.

Then they came to a fork in the pathway.

"Now what do we do?" Ingrid said.

Mark pointed to the left path that was obviously more traveled.

"I'm pretty sure when I came here last time that we went this way," he said.

He wandered a little way down the path on the left. As he walked, he thought he heard voices of the others searching for Kyle. He didn't want to get caught in the forest alone so he returned to the head of the fork, where Ingrid was waiting.

"Put Chee Chee down on the ground and see which way he goes," Ingrid suggested.

"Good idea," Mark responded. He put Chee Chee down and said "Chee Chee, find Kyle."

Chee Chee started off towards the path on the right. Mark followed. Ingrid hesitated for a minute, then she followed Mark and Chee Chee further into the forest.

This path was much more difficult than the first one. Fallen trees, branches and vines were scattered across the path waiting to trip the careless walker. Mark no longer searched for forest animals; he kept his eyes trained on the ground.

"I hope Chee Chee knows where he's going," Ingrid muttered.

"He does," Mark reassured her.

He jumped on to a branch that lay in his way and jumped down on the other side.

"Yuck!" he exclaimed.

"What happened?" Ingrid asked.

"Mud," was Mark's reply. "All over my shoes and socks."

Chee Chee ran forward, clearly very sure of the way. Sometimes he would run forward as far as his leash would allow and then come back as if urging them to hurry.

"Only Kyle would choose to come out here!" Ingrid muttered stomping through the underbrush.

They were so focused on the ground that they were surprised when they felt the warmth of the sun on the back of their necks. Mark looked up. They had followed the path out of the forest into a clearing. A river bed lay in front of them, dry except for a thin trail of water that meandered through the rocks in the river.

"This must be part of the Guacharo River," Mark said, looking back at Ingrid. "It's the main river that runs through this part of the Arima valley."

"What's up with Chee Chee?" Ingrid asked.

Chee Chee had stopped moving forward and was running excitedly around something on the ground.

Mark walked over to Chee Chee and picked up the object. It was the small telescope that Kyle had been given on their adventure with the pirates at Port Royal.

"It's Kyle's. This means he was here," Mark paused, his lip trembled. "It also means he's in trouble. He would never have dropped this by mistake."

"I'm scared," Ingrid admitted, "let's get help. We have proof now that this is the way he came."

"We've come this far," Mark insisted. "Whatever has happened, if we go all the way back to get help it might be too late. We have to go on. He can't be far."

Mark pocketed the telescope and started forward, but Chee Chee would not move, in spite of Mark's tugging on the leash. The monkey stayed rooted to the spot where he had found the telescope.

"Come on, Chee Chee, let's go," Mark said.

"Maybe he lost the scent," Ingrid said.

"I doubt it," Mark replied, "Kyle must be somewhere around here. Let's call him."

Mark cupped his hand around his mouth and called loudly, "KYLE". He turned to face the opposite direction, cupped his mouth again and shouted, "KYLE". He began turning around in a circle, shouting "KYLE". If he spun fast enough when he shouted, he could hear his voice rushing past his ears like a bus speeding by on the highway. He spun faster and faster, enjoying the sound.

"Mark, stop playing the fool," Ingrid cried.

But Mark ignored her. He kept spinning until, finally he was dizzy and he stopped, disoriented and stumbling around a bit. He took a step to the side to steady himself and suddenly he felt the earth dissolving from underneath him as he fell into a deep hole. He tried to grab on to the vines and brush that had covered the hole, but they fell into the hole with him.

He dropped with a thump at the bottom. He was dazed for a few seconds and then slowly and gingerly he got to his feet. He hadn't hurt himself although the hole was very deep. He looked up the sides of the hole; they were very steep and he couldn't climb out.

He heard Ingrid up above.

"Mark!" she screamed.

Then her voice sounded much closer as if she were directly above the hole.

"Mark, are you okay?"

From his prison beneath the earth, Mark yelled, "Ingrid, run! Get help! Run!"

Chapter 5

Down the Rabbit Hole

Mark was surrounded in darkness. A thin stream of light came from above; a little sunlight that seeped down to the bottom. Since he could not climb up, Mark started searching for another way out. He used his hands to feel his way along the walls of the hole until his eyes grew accustomed to the dark. He soon discovered that it was quite large and was actually a small cave. He felt his way to a doorway in the wall, his heart filled with hope that there was another way out.

He went through the archway and he saw a slit of light in the distance. Then his hopes fell as he realised that the outer cave was blocked by a large wrought iron gate, blocking his way to the rest of the cave.

He didn't have much time to consider this new problem before he heard a rustling sound behind him followed by a girl's scream. He ran back into the main cave and was very surprised to see Ingrid hurtling through the roof. He ran over to help her up from where she had fallen.

"Are you okay?" he asked.

"Yeah, I think so," Ingrid replied, dazed from the fall and everything that was happening.

"What are you doing down here?" Mark asked.

Ingrid looked sheepish. "I was trying to figure out what to do. A man came out of the forest. He ran at me, shouting. I was so frightened, I forgot about the hole. I stepped back to get away from him and fell in here."

"What did the man look like? Maybe he was one of the rangers looking for Kyle."

"I don't think so. He called us 'meddling kids'. I figure he must be a poacher."

"Where's Chee Chee?" Mark asked.

"I don't know. He tried to warn me that the man was coming and then he disappeared," Ingrid replied.

"He tried to warn me too. That's why he wouldn't go any further after we found Kyle's telescope."

"Do you think this guy captured Kyle?"

"I don't know," Mark replied.

The children heard footsteps and stopped talking. Mark took Ingrid's hand and guided her towards the big iron gate so that they could see who was coming. A man strode towards the metal gate. As he came closer, the children saw that he was dragging something heavy behind him.

"Is that the man you saw?" Mark whispered.

"I think so," Ingrid replied.

The man reached the gate of the prison and stuck his face between the bars. The face was brown and creased like a piece of leather that had been in the sun too long. But the thing that alarmed Mark most was the long scar on his right cheek. It was shaped like a lightning bolt and made him look very fierce. Mark and Ingrid cowered under his malevolent stare.

The man took out some keys, opened the metal gate and threw the bundle that he was carrying into the cave with the other children.

"I'll be back when I figure out what to do with you." He slammed the gate shut, turned the key and stomped off.

The bundle groaned and pulled itself into a sitting position. It was Kyle.

"Kyle, are you okay?" Mark ran over to where Kyle had landed.

"Yeah," he replied weakly, "he didn't hurt me; I just hurt my arm when I fell in here the first time." He peered through the dim light at Ingrid and Mark. "What are you doing here?"

"We came looking for you, stupid," Ingrid said angrily. "What were you thinking about, running off like that?"

"I don't know," Kyle replied, "I just wanted to catch the lizard. I followed it into the forest and the forest was so cool. I didn't realise how far I had gone. Then I fell in the trap."

"Who's this guy? Did he say anything to you?" Mark asked.

"He's a poacher. I think he's the one taking the oilbirds from the Dunston's Cave."

"Wait, what's that noise?" Mark interrupted.

He held one hand up in the air, tipping his head in the direction of the metal gate.

The three children looked towards the gate and saw Chee Chee walking down the passageway towards them. He stopped in front of the locked gate.

"Chee Chee!" Mark exclaimed.

Chee Chee dropped something through the bars. Mark walked over and, to his great surprise, he discovered that the monkey had dropped a ring with two keys on to the floor of the cave.

"Good boy! You got the keys? How did you manage that?" Kyle was beside himself with excitement.

"He must have snuck them out of the poacher's pocket," Mark replied. "Come on, let's get out of here quickly. It won't be long before he discovers his keys are missing."

Mark picked up the keys, pushed his hand through the gate and twisted his arm around so that he could put the key in the lock and turn it. After a few tries, he opened the lock.

The children filed quietly out of the cave. Kyle took the keys from Mark and locked the door behind them.

"It might slow him down a bit if he can't open the gate to see if we are there," Kyle murmured. He put the keys into his pocket.

Chee Chee ran ahead of the children and they followed him. He went further into the tunnel and then he made a left turn down another tunnel. The ceiling of the tunnel was low and Mark had to bend at some points to get through without hitting his head.

"This isn't the way the man took me," Kyle said.

"And that's a good thing," Ingrid replied, "We're trying to get *away* from him, remember?"

"What's that smell?" Mark wrinkled his nose.

"Ewwww!" Kyle exclaimed, "It smells like something died in here."

"And what's that noise? It sounds like someone's crying," Ingrid exclaimed covering her ears to block out the loud cries coming from deep in the cave.

Chee Chee continued moving forward despite the assault on their noses and ears. Gradually, the roof of the tunnel got higher and Mark no longer had to bend his head. The tunnel widened into a cave. Mark was the first to enter.

"Watch out, it's …."

"AHHHH!" Kyle stepped into the cave, slipped and fell with a smack on his bottom.

"…slippery," Mark tried not to laugh.

Kyle got to his feet and tried to clean his hands and the seat of his pants.

"What's this stuff anyway?" he asked, raising his hands to his nose.

Before anyone could respond, Ingrid screamed. She tugged on Kyle's shirt and pointed behind them. High up in the roof of the cave, two reddish brown eyes stared curiously at the children.

"Wha … What's that?" Ingrid stammered.

"It must be an oilbird," Mark replied, "we must be in the back of Dunston's Cave. He paused. "Which means that the stuff on the ground is probably bird poop."

"Oh no!" Kyle said.

"Oh yes," Ingrid replied, "and boy do you stink!" Her laughter was short lived and she screamed again as the bird she had seen launched itself in her direction. The children watched the bird fly over their heads, turn and disappear into the depths of the cave. They could hear quite a bit of activity in the cave ahead. It sounded as if a number of birds were taking flight, but none of them came close to the children.

They heard footsteps pounding down the tunnel behind them.

"He's coming," Kyle whispered.

Chee Chee ran further into the cave. Mark grabbed Kyle's hand and pulled him forward, forcing him into a run. Ingrid followed. The children moved as quickly as they could although the floor of the cave was slippery, covered in the oilbirds' dung. They heard the man's footsteps getting closer.

"You have nowhere to run," he shouted menacingly from behind them.

"He's right," Mark said, "Look!"

Several meters ahead of them, they could see the wall of the cave. Light came from the roof and it seemed that the only way out was up.

Chapter 6

Hunted

"We're trapped!" Kyle exclaimed.

"We can't be," Mark replied, "There must be another entrance to this cave."

As they approached the cave wall, Chee Chee seemed to just disappear into the cave wall. Mark, who was first behind Chee Chee, looked all about, trying to figure out where the monkey had gone. He was about to call his pet when he noticed a small tunnel on his right. The entrance was hidden in the shadows.

Mark looked over his shoulder to make sure that Ingrid and Kyle saw where he was going and then he stepped sideways into the tunnel, following Chee Chee as quickly as he could.

The tunnel sloped upwards. The children climbed following Chee Chee into the sunlight ahead. They stepped out and found themselves once more in the crisp, fresh air of the rainforest.

"Woah, where are we now?" Kyle exclaimed rubbing his eyes.

The children had stumbled out of the cave into bright daylight. Mark glanced around. They were once again on the grassy bank of the Guacharo River. The river bed lay in front of them.

"Don't know," Mark panted. "Keep running."

They ran through the grass and began to cross the dry river bed. Ingrid tripped on one of the rocks scattered throughout the river bed and fell.

"Owwww!" she cried out, holding her leg.

Kyle looked back. He stopped, grabbed her hand and yanked her to her feet.

"Don't be a baby, come on," he urged.

"Who you calling baby?" Ingrid pulled her hand out of Kyle's. "You're the one who got us in this mess, wandering off. I wish I never came looking for you."

Mark interjected, "Will you two cut it out. We have to keep moving, the poacher's right behind us."

"There's no one following us," Ingrid said. "Stop, listen."

The boys stopped and looked back towards the cave's entrance. They held their breaths and listened. Everything seemed to stand still with them. Ingrid was right; there was no movement at the mouth of the cave. Mark was finally able to take in his surroundings. He looked up at the sky, feeling that something wasn't quite right. The sky was a brilliant blue with just a few misty clouds over the tree tops. The air smelled fresh and clean. The grass they walked in was damp, but there was no sign of water in the river. The sun filtered through the leaves of the trees on the other side of the river bed. The droplets of water on the leaves fractured the light into strange colours; yellows, blues and violets.

"That's really strange," Kyle said. "He was right behind us, why would he let us get away?"

He walked over to the other side of the river bed and collapsed on to the grass. Mark could see that he was exhausted from his ordeal with the poacher, so he was very surprised when Kyle stood right back up.

"The grass is wet!" he said. "Did it rain?"

"No," Ingrid replied, "Must be dew!"

"Dew?" Kyle said scornfully, "in the middle of the afternoon? Please!"

"It's not rain," Ingrid insisted. "There are no clouds and the river is bone dry." She paused, thinking, "which is real weird because I swear it was wet when we walked by it before."

"I think it's morning," Mark said, finally figuring out what had been bothering him. "I remember that the Guacharo River runs north to south, so that way must be north." He pointed ahead of him along the river in the direction of the mountains. "And so, that way," he pointed to his right, "is east, and the sun is in the east, so it must be morning."

"It can't be morning?" Ingrid said. "We weren't in the cave that long, it couldn't be."

"I hate to agree with Ingrid, Mr. Boy Scout, but it's not morning," Kyle said.

"I just remember from when I came up here last time. I remember them talking about the way the river ran, down from the Northern Range. I know it sounds crazy, but look how bright the sky is. I wonder if Chee Chee has taken us into the …"

Mark's sentence was interrupted by something flying past his ear. He looked around in time to see an arrow plow into a nearby tree and stick there, the end of the arrow vibrating from the impact.

"Where did that come from?" Kyle shouted.

Ingrid looked around towards the forest, "I don't know? I think it was over …" She too was interrupted as another arrow flew from the direction of the trees.

"Duck!" Kyle warned, grabbing Ingrid's arm and pulling her down on to the wet grass. Mark didn't need another warning. He dove into the grass as well, just as another arrow whizzed by.

"What's going on now?" Ingrid moaned. "How could Ms. Isles bring us to such a dangerous place on a field trip?"

"I don't think we're on *that* field trip anymore," Mark whispered. "I think that Chee Chee has taken us time traveling again."

"How does he *do* that?" said Ingrid.

"Shhh!" Kyle whispered urgently. "Let's see if we can make it to those rocks over there."

The three children ran to take cover behind some boulders in the river. They heard another arrow hit a tree on the other side of the forest.

"Whoever it is isn't aiming at us," Ingrid said.

Mark looked for Chee Chee. He assumed that the monkey had followed them behind the rocks, but the monkey had run off towards the forest. Another arrow flew in the monkey's direction. They were flying by more frequently now, clearly meant to hit Chee Chee.

The children watched with horror as Chee Chee dodged one arrow that hit very close to its mark. He looked in the children's direction, then leapt into the nearest tree and disappeared into the forest.

A few seconds later, the children heard running footsteps. A boy came into view. Mark guessed that he was about 13, two or three years older than they were. He had a bow in his left hand and a quiver with arrows in the back of his pants.

The boy ran nimbly along the river bed picking up his spent arrows and stuffing them into his tattered quiver. He bent to get one not far from where the children hid. Kyle gave a sharp intake of breath when he saw the boy's face. It was scarred with a lightening shaped mark right below his eye, just like the one on the face of the poacher who had held him in Dunston's Cave.

The boy looked over to the rocks where the children hid. His eyes narrowed as he tried to focus. The children held their breaths and kept as still as possible in their hiding place. Then they all heard a rustle in the trees. The boy turned in the direction of the noise, stuffed the last arrow into his quiver and ran off in the direction of the noise.

Chapter 7

Animal Rescue

The children emerged from behind the rock.

"Did you see that scar?" Kyle exclaimed. "It looked exactly like the one the poacher had; in the same place."

"Yeah. I'm not sure it was on the same cheek, though." Mark replied.

"It was," Kyle insisted. "I spent more time with him. I'll never forget that scar."

"It must be his father or something," Ingrid said.

"It could be the poacher," Mark offered, knowing that the others would think he was crazy.

"The poacher!" Kyle laughed again.

"But he's a boy," Ingrid said, "The poacher's a man. We would have to be … Oh! I get it, you still think we're in the past."

"Yes," Mark said. "That would explain why it's morning and why the old poacher didn't follow us out of the cave."

"It makes sense," Ingrid said, "well, it makes sense if you've had the adventures we've had."

"True," Kyle exclaimed. "Another adventure! I wonder how far back we are this time."

"Not too far, if this boy is the poacher," Ingrid began, "maybe 30 or 40 years. He looked about as old as my father."

"Can we worry about that later?" Mark said. "We have to find Chee Chee."

He started towards the forest and his friends followed. They entered the forest at the same place the boy had and they discovered a slightly

72

worn path. The children were hot from running, and walking under the forest canopy was like entering an air conditioned room after sitting in the sun. They picked their way along the path in silence, deep in thought.

After a minute, they arrived at a fork in the path. They stopped and looked at each other.

"Which way do we go now?" Ingrid asked.

"I don't know," Mark replied with a sigh.

"I'm tired," Ingrid said, sitting down on the grass.

Kyle nudged her with his foot. "We have to keep moving," he said, "we can't let Chee Chee and that boy get too far ahead of us."

"Don't kick me," Ingrid retorted.

"I didn't kick you. Anyway, let's go that way, it seems more disturbed than the other path."

He pointed to the left.

"Who's being a boy scout now?" Ingrid replied pointing to the right.. "I think we should go that way."

"You always have to disagree with me!"

"Because I'm always right and you're always wrong!"

Mark lost his composure. "Will you two stop? I can't take it any more. Chee Chee is lost; some boy is trying to shoot him with arrows and all you two can do is argue!"

He paused. "Well, I'm going to look for him," and with that he stomped off, choosing the path on the left.

There was silence behind him. Mark guessed that his friends were shocked by his outburst but he didn't look back. He tramped along the path, his anger dissipating a little with each step. He didn't want to call out to Chee Chee and alert the boy with the arrows. He hoped that Chee Chee would come to him so that they could escape together. He walked through the forest, trying to come up with a plan.

He found himself in an area of the forest where the undergrowth was thicker and the air was darker than where they had been before. It was quiet, and reminded him of a scene from a scary movie right before a wild animal jumped out and attacked the hero.

Then he heard a sound, four soft whistles, each one higher pitched than the one before. Mark had never heard anything quite like it, but he imagined it might be like the sound that dogs heard from the silent whistles that couldn't be heard by humans. Mark was terrified. He stopped and looked in the direction of the sound but he saw nothing. His heart thumped loudly in his chest.

"Toot! Toot! Toot! Toot!"

This time the whistle came from behind him. He whipped around and saw the melody maker.

The bird was on a branch high in a tree not far from where Mark stood. It bent its head into a large fern that was growing on the same tree. It seemed to be drinking or eating from the leaves of the fern. It looked like a turkey and Mark's first thought was 'A turkey? So high up in a tree? I'm sure they don't fly!'

He stepped forward tentatively to get a closer look and the bird didn't fly away. Now he could see that the legs that extended from its glossy black feathered body were bright red. It lifted its head from the fern and showed its face which was a brilliant blue. Mark decided that the bird was definitely not a turkey.

He heard another low whistle behind him. He turned. This time he spotted the bright blue face of another bird between the trees. Then he heard a third one. Before he could find that one, the first one that he spotted lifted its head and made a sound like a duck quacking. About five or six birds moved as if they were one, stretching their wings, rising out of the trees and flying away.

Mark turned to see what had made the birds fly away and found himself face to face with a very sharp looking arrow. At the other end of the arrow stood the boy who they had seen earlier.

"Who are you?" he asked.

Mark said nothing, unsure of how to explain that they came from the boy's future.

The boy didn't wait long for an answer.

"Well, you're coming with me," he said. He had a coil of rope slung over his left shoulder. He took this and deftly tied Mark's hands firmly behind his back. He held the end of the rope and prodded Mark in the back with the arrow.

"Walk," he commanded, in a voice much deeper and more commanding than Mark expected from a boy his age.

Mark obeyed, walking in the direction that the arrow pointed.

The boy guided Mark back to the path and they followed it to the fork where Mark had left his friends. Ingrid and Kyle were sitting on the ground tied to each other and then to a tree.

"I found your friend. You guys tramp around the forest like elephants. Now, tell me about the monkey. I've never seen one like it before. I want it for my collection."

"Collection? Chee Chee will never be in anyone's collection!" Mark exclaimed.

"Chee Chee, eh? That's his name? Well, I can track anything in this forest and I *will* find that monkey.

"Come on."

The boy untied the rope that bound Kyle and Ingrid to the tree and pointed the children in the direction of the path that led to the right. They walked one behind the other, Ingrid, Kyle then Mark. They stumbled along, hampered by the ropes that attached them.

"What's your name?" Mark asked.

"None of your business," was the reply.

"How'd you get the scar?" Ingrid asked.

"Wrestling with an armadillo," the boy replied with a sly smile. "I sneaked up on it and he jumped up on to my face. He scratched me real deep on my cheek but I held on to him. Guess who won the fight? And I was only seven then."

"You killed it?" Ingrid asked, her eyes wide.

"Nah. Just added it to my collection."

"A regular 'Crocodile Dundee'," Ingrid said.

"What?" the boy's face was blank.

"That movie doesn't exist yet," Kyle said.

"Forget it. How can you boast about fighting a defenseless animal like an armadillo?" Ingrid asked.

"You ask too many questions." The boy gave Mark a little shove. "Shut up and keep moving."

They continued without talking. The only sounds they heard were the calls of the birds in the forest. Mark kept his ears peeled for the piping sounds of the turkey-like bird he had seen earlier, but he didn't hear them. He wondered if they were just smart enough to stay far away from the boy with his bow and arrows.

As they walked, the forest noises seemed to grow increasingly louder. After a while, it sounded as if there were a lot of animals congregated and they were all squawking, chirping, cackling and growling at the same time.

Mark remembered reading the word 'cacophony' in a book or a poem and he thought that the word was a great description for the mix of noises they were hearing.

Mark looked behind him. Their captor was frowning and seemed to be quite upset by the sounds he heard ahead of him.

"What's all that noise," Kyle asked.

"Shhhh!" the boy replied.

They passed a crude wooden sign.

"Jack's Jungle. Keep Out," Ingrid read aloud. "Are you Jack?"

Intent on moving forward, the boy didn't reply.

"Look at that!" Ingrid exclaimed and stopped walking suddenly. Mark and Kyle plowed into her and struggled to keep their balance.

"Watch out!" Kyle started. He was about to complain some more but he stopped when he saw what was ahead.

"Woah!" he exclaimed.

In front of them was a large clearing about the size of a basketball court. No grass grew on the ground at all and the trees had all been cut down. Inside the cleared area there were about 20 cages of various shapes and sizes. Some were stacked untidily on top of others. The floor of the cages was covered in old newspaper soiled by animal droppings and inside the cages were dirty bowls and old white ice cream containers.

There were no animals in the cages. The cage doors were all wide open and a number of animals congregated in the middle of the corral, confused and dazed at the prospect of freedom after a long period of confinement.

Mark tried to identify some of the animals. There were two parrots, three large turtles, and a green scaly iguana. He also spotted the hard shell and bands of an armadillo and he wondered if it was the same one that had scratched the boy's face years before.

Jack dropped the rope he had used to guide Ingrid, Mark and Kyle and ran towards the animals.

"What's that?" Kyle asked, pointing his chin in the direction of a small animal. It had a rounded back that made it look like it was hunched over, small ears and a very short tail.

"Agouti," Mark replied.

"Gouti?" Kyle repeated.

Mark laughed, "No. Agouti. One word."

"Oooh that one over there looks like a rat with four ears. Disgusting!" Ingrid exclaimed.

"It's a manicou," Mark replied. "They eat them here in Trinidad. Tastes good."

"And look, a snake!" Ingrid shivered. Then she added. "I hope they all escape. This boy is mean!"

Jack moved frantically among the animals, waving his arms and shooing them towards their cages. On seeing him, the animals seemed to come to their senses. They ran, walked, waddled, slithered and flew towards the forest and disappeared. He was able to recapture some of the slower animals, the turtles and the poor armadillo, but most of his captives escaped.

The boy managed to catch one of the turkey-like birds that Mark had seen in the forest. As he held it in his arms, it beat its wide wings furiously. Mark watched, rooting silently for the bird. He almost clapped when the bird worked its way loose from its captor's arms, but Jack made a desperate grab and took hold of the bird again. It worked even harder to escape. It wriggled in the boy's arms until its wings were free. Jack still held the long red legs, but the bird flapped its wings again. The bird rose into the air and Mark opened his eyes in amazement as Jack was lifted a few inches off the ground. The boy screamed and let go. The bird's wings made a drumming sound as it escaped into the surrounding trees.

"My Pawi!" the boy wailed.

Mark felt a tugging behind him. He turned and exclaimed softly.

"Chee Chee! You're okay? Good boy!"

Chee Chee pulled and tugged at the ropes around Mark's hands until they came lose. Then Mark untied the others. Jack didn't notice that his human captives were also escaping. He seemed to have forgotten about them as he tried to recapture as many animals as possible.

Mark whispered "Let's go!"

The children ran down the path, back the way they had come, heading towards the river bed.

They hadn't run very far when they heard a shout. "It's you! You meddling monkey. You let them out!"

There was a tramping through the forest as the boy ran full pelt in pursuit of Mark and his friends.

The children began to run. Chee Chee went ahead of them. He led them away from the path and deep into the forest. Mark was really happy to have Chee Chee leading them again, and he followed him, confident that the monkey would lead them to safety.

Chapter 8

Chee Chee's plan

The children followed Chee Chee into the forest's undergrowth, running faster than they ever had in their lives. They could hear the boy behind them.

"You can't get away from me!" he called out to them. "I must have that monkey!"

Ingrid started to lag behind, her leg hurting from her fall in the river bed. Mark grabbed her hand, urging her along as they sped through the undergrowth trying to keep up with Chee Chee.

"He's catching up," Kyle panted. "We're not going to make it. Where's Chee Chee going?"

"Not sure," Mark replied, "but keep following."

Mark hoped he sounded more confident than he felt. They seemed to be going away from the Dunston's Cave rather than towards it and he was beginning to feel a little unsure about Chee Chee's plan.

"He's zig-zaging. Trying to lose Jack," Ingrid said.

Mark realised that she was right. Every now and then, the monkey would make a sharp tack to the right or the left. It didn't seem to be working. Jack saw them each time and kept up his pursuit. Mark was so caught up in his worry that he almost missed Chee Chee's last zig. The monkey made a swift left turn. The children followed and found themselves in front of a cave. Its mouth was just large enough for them to enter one by one. When they were all inside,

Chee Chee went back to the opening of the cave and peeped out. Mark looked out as well.

The mouth of the cave was very well disguised by shrubs and vines and Jack went running straight past it. A few seconds later, the children heard a scream. Chee Chee scampered out of the cave and they followed him.

Just beyond the cave, the path narrowed. There was a steep cliff on one side. The children moved slowly, picking their way along the edge. Jack, who had been running, had slipped off of the path. The children could see him holding on to some branches on the side of the cliff.

"Ahhhh!" Jack screamed again as the branch he was holding broke and he slipped down a little further. There was a valley of trees about 100 feet below him. He would be badly hurt, perhaps even killed if he fell to the bottom.

Ingrid looked over the edge of the gully and gasped.

"What are we going to do?" she wailed, "we have to help him!"

"Look. What's Chee Chee doing?" Kyle pointed at the monkey.

Chee Chee was in one of the trees on the edge of the gully. It was a flamboyant tree, just like the ones in Independence Square in St. Kitts. The tree was planted near the edge of the gully, and its roots were visible down the sides of the gully like ropes holding the soil intact. The branches hung well over the cliff.

Chee Chee ran to the end of the longest branch. He was pulling a long thick vine behind him. The children watched as he wrapped the vine around a strong tree branch. He swung it into the valley below so that it hung very close to

Jack's hands. Jack was looking down at the drop below him and didn't see what was happening above him.

"Jack!" Mark shouted, "Grab the vine!"

Jack looked up and saw the children at the top of the cliff and the vine hanging down in front of him.

"I can't," he cried, "I can't let go."

"You have to," Kyle shouted back jumping up and down at the top of the cliff, "Chee Chee is trying to save you!"

"What if he drops me?" The children could hear the terror in Jack's voice. "I tried to capture him. Suppose he drops me."

"Chee Chee would never hurt anyone," Mark said. "You have no choice. Grab the vine."

"Thanks, but no thanks," Jack called out and he started to climb up the side of the cliff.

"I can't watch!" Ingrid covered her eyes.

Jack held on to a root and groaned as he pulled himself up. He reached up and held on to another plant. That plant didn't hold. Mark watched in horror as the entire plant, leaves and root came out in Jack's hand. Jack screamed and grabbed at the vine that Chee Chee had lowered for him. The vine straightened, stretched to its full length with the boy's weight. He swung in the air, twisting in small arcs, back and forth, slower and slower until he stopped. He clung desperately to the vine with both hands.

"Climb up," Kyle called, still dancing around at the top of the cliff, unable to contain his excitement. "Climb up!"

Jack began to pull himself up the vine, one hand over the other. Chee Chee had tied it securely to the branch of the tree. They all watched as Jack crawled slowly to the top.

"He's going to be okay," Kyle nudged Ingrid, "Open your eyes. Look!"

Ingrid lowered her hands from her eyes just in time to see Jack hoist himself up into the branches of the flamboyant tree.

"How will he get out of the tree?" she asked, but she need not have worried. Once Jack was safe, he crawled his way from across the branch and shimmied down the tree trunk.

Mark and Kyle ran to the bottom of the tree. Chee Chee climbed down and sat at their feet.

"You alright?" Mark asked.

"Yeah, thanks," Jack replied. He looked over at Chee Chee. "That's some monkey," he said shaking his head, "that was unbelievable."

"Yep," Mark replied, "he's pretty amazing."

"He saved my life ... even though I was trying to capture him, he saved my life." Jack looked over the cliff where he had fallen and stepped back; he shook his head and repeated, "He saved my life."

Jack started to walk away. He was limping. Mark could see that he was badly bruised from his tumble down the cliff. Suddenly the boy didn't look quite so scary. Mark felt a little sorry for him.

"Let us help you," Mark said, walking over to him. He took the boy's arm and put it around his shoulder. "Lean on me."

Kyle did the same on the other side. Jack was so exhausted from his experience he didn't protest. In this manner, they went back to the Guacharo River, Chee Chee, the three boys and Ingrid walking behind.

Chapter 9

Back to Reality

They took Jack back to the place where his cages had been. He had been very quiet on the walk back and seemed even more dejected now. He sat down at the foot of one of the trees that corralled his clearing.

"Will you be okay?" Mark asked. "Should we take you to your mother?"

"I'll be okay," Jack replied. "I just need to sit here for a while. You guys head on home. I ..."

Mark, Ingrid and Kyle looked at him expectantly, waiting for him to finish his sentence, but he didn't. Instead he snarled at them. "I said go on home, before I change my mind and lock up your monkey."

He wasn't very convincing, but Mark was very disappointed that Jack would speak to them in that manner after all that they had been through.

Kyle looked at Mark's crest fallen face. He put his arm around his friend and said, "Come on, Mark. We're not welcome here, let's go back."

Chee Chee had already started down the path. He stopped and looked back at them as if to say "Are you coming or not?"

The children retraced their steps to the dry river bed and stopped outside of the entrance of the cave. None of them made a move to enter.

"What do you think we're going to find in there?" Kyle said.

"I have no idea," Mark replied.

"We have to go back…I mean forward," Ingrid said, "and this has to be the way."

"Yeah, but will that poacher still be chasing us? Will he remember today? What will we find?" Kyle rattled the questions off quickly.

"I have no idea," Mark repeated, peering cautiously into the mouth of the cave. "Here's the plan, I'll go in first, see what's happening and then I'll call you all to follow."

"Sounds good to me," Kyle said, sitting down on the grass outside the cave.

"We can't let him go in alone!" said Ingrid.

"I'll be fine with Chee Chee," Mark replied.

Mark entered the cave with Chee Chee. When the monkey noticed that Ingrid and Kyle weren't coming, he ran back to the mouth of the cave and chattered at them.

Mark came back and stuck his head out. "It seems that we're meant to stick together. Chee

Chee has never led us wrong, so I guess we'll have to trust him again."

They all entered the cave tentatively, ready at any moment to run back out if the poacher showed his face. There was no sign of him. They walked all the way back through the narrow passageway, into the larger cavern, through the wrought iron gate that was wide open and back below the hole through which they had all fallen.

"Now what?" Kyle asked, turning around in the small space.

"Shhh! Listen!" said Ingrid.

The three children stood stock still in the hole. This time they all heard what Ingrid had heard, voices outside, near the hole.

They started to shout altogether, "Down here. We're down here. Help! Help!"

Seconds later someone pushed their head down the hole and called out, "Is someone down there!"

The children were almost faint with relief. "Yes, yes, we fell in. We need help!"

The rescue work was very swift. The rangers dropped a rope down into the cave and pulled the children out. Ingrid was the first to be hoisted up. The rangers cheered and one guide hugged her when she arrived at the top, dirty and tired. They were surprised to see a girl appear as they had been sent to look for a boy.

"He's still down there," she told them, "two more."

Soon they were all out. One of the guides was confused, "They told us one child was missing, how come there are three of you?"

Mark and Ingrid looked sheepishly at the ground. Ingrid spoke up, "It's my fault; I made Mark come looking for Kyle."

"You?" said Kyle, turning to look at Ingrid, his dark brown eyes opened wide. "I thought you hated me, why did you come looking for me?"

"I was worried ... if you got hurt or lost, who would I have to argue with." she dropped her voice and added "Besides, I don't hate you, not at all."

Mark looked at Kyle and nudged him.

Kyle put his hands behind his back and looked at his feet. "Thanks," he said softly, "and I don't hate you either. ... well, not really."

The guides questioned the children about where they had been. They weren't sure how to answer. They couldn't very well say that they had been captured by a poacher and then traveled into the past and rescued the poacher when he was a child!

Chee Chee found his own way out of the underground caves. One of the rangers spotted the monkey and stepped forward.

"Hey," he said, "I remember meeting a monkey like you when I was a young boy!" He dropped his voice. "It kind of changed my life. Maybe I'll tell you the story on the way back to the main house."

Chee Chee scampered over to him and the man stooped down to tickle the monkey's chin. To the children's amazement, the man had a lightening shaped scar on his right cheek.

"So that's what it was all about," Mark muttered loud enough for Ingrid and Kyle to hear.

"Yes," Kyle replied, "Like you said, Chee Chee's one amazing monkey!"

Where It All Happened

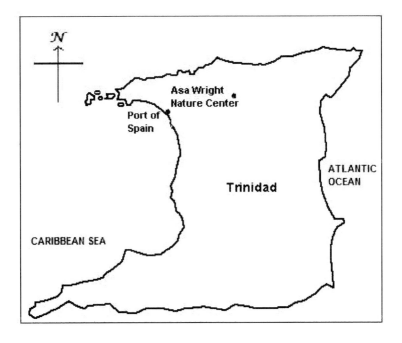

What's True and What's Not

Are the Asa Wright Nature Center and Dunston's Cave real places? They certainly are. The Asa Wright Nature Center (AWNC) was created in 1967 to protect the plants and animals in the Arima Valley in Trinidad so that everyone can enjoy and learn about them. It was one of the first nature centers to be established in the Caribbean.

The Center's main facilities are located on a former cocoa-coffee-citrus plantation, previously known as the Spring Hill Estate.

Dunston's Cave is a cave located on the grounds of the AWNC.

Do oilbirds really exist? Yes, they do. Oilbirds are the only <u>nocturnal</u> fruit eating birds in the world. Those that are located in Dunston's Cave are perhaps the easiest colony to view in the world.

Do turkeys fly? The answer to that question is: it depends. Turkeys can fly, however, domestic turkeys, those that live on farms, don't fly because they are usually too fat. Wild turkeys eat on the ground, but they sleep in tress at night.

Is the Pawi Pipile a real bird? Yes, it is and it's endangered so if you see one, consider yourself very lucky.

About the CAS

Trapped in Dunston's Cave is book three in the Caribbean Adventure Series. Here are the first two:

Adventure at Brimstone Hill: Join Mark, Kyle and Ingrid on their very first adventure as they follow Chee Chee, their mischievous monkey through a secret passage at the Brimstone Hill Fortress National Park in St. Kitts. They find themselves transported to the 18th century, captured as spies and thrown into a fierce battle for this famous fort.

Pirates at Port Royal: Port Royal was destroyed by an earthquake in 1692, but that doesn't stop Mark, Kyle and their pet monkey Chee Chee from having an adventure there during their summer in Jamaica. The children once again find themselves in the past. This time they team up with Henry Morgan, a famous pirate, on an adventure that takes them to Venezuela where they have to destroy a fleet of Spanish ships to save their lives.

CPSIA information can be obtained at www.ICGtesting.com
Printed in the USA
BVOW02s0924010616

450272BV00004B/15/P